Milkweed

Also By Michael R. Milano

Conversations and Poetry
Mulberry Doon: Stories and Poetry

Milkweed

MICHAEL R. MILANO

FCP

Full Court Press
Englewood Cliffs, New Jersey

Published in the United States of America
by Full Court Press, 601 Palisade Avenue,
Englewood Cliffs, NJ 07632
fullcourtpressnj.com

ISBN 978-1-938812-77-4
Library of Congress Catalog No. 2016942717

*Book design by Barry Sheinkopf for Bookshapers
(bookshapers.com)*

Cover art courtesy thinkstock.com

Colophon by Liz Sedlack

DEDICATION

To Drs. Steven Frier, George Leber,
Dmitri Nemirovsky, and others who have,
with great skill, kept me around to write this book.

ACKNOWLEDGMENTS

To my inspiration and most careful critic, Patty, and our fellow poetry readers: Bob Ghiradella, Addie Wijnen, Jeff Fish, Jon Long, and Monica Hodges, all of whom encouraged me. My old college roommate, Paul Murphy, lent a keen eye for detail and correct English. Barry Sheinkopf did the yeoman's work of publishing and helping with covers and artwork. My thanks to all.

TABLE OF CONTENTS

Chapter Five

(Observations about Nature, personal moments, and love poems.)

Chapter Six

("Dusk" and "I Want to Leave You" are included from prior publications because they fit so well with the bittersweet of love and loss. They are the soul of the book.)

Chapter One

WHO AM I

Phillip
Ruth
Jeremy
Lorita
Maxine
Chondra

Act 1, Scene 1. Phillip and Ruth's apartment. 8:00 p.m.

Ruth: Well, we had a little dinner, and your nose has been in the newspapers ever since.

Phillip: I'm tired, and I have a terrible headache. Sure I love you, and you're beautiful. Never doubted it.

Ruth: Look at me. [Fifteen seconds pass, and Ruth stamps her foot] Your wife is begging, and all you do is look at that newspaper. [She grabs the newspaper].

Phillip: Look Ruth, I'm sorry. Tomorrow is Friday night, and we'll do candles, soft music, nice wine; everything. [Gestures] . I'll make it real special and different.

Ruth: I don't need all that. I just want to feel you're there. [Pause].

You know, your mother told me [he drops his head] that this happened to her, and I even think it happened to my parents. [Sniffling] So I'm scared. I don't want candles and soft music. I need you there, listening to me. Wanting me. . . .

Phillip: I know a guy at work I could score some weed from. It'll be like the old days of Jefferson Airplane and Janis Joplin. I want you to be more like Janice, or even Gracie Slick. They took what they wanted. Fearless. Well, honey, the love is there. Wait till Friday night.

Ruth: Tomorrow, tomorrow. Always tomorrow.

Act 1, Scene 2: A Chelsea bar–restaurant table.
Phillip and Jeremy at the bar.

Phillip: What a life! Always running up hill. Our big victory is one night every two weeks to get drunk together.

Jeremy: At least we're free tonight and don't have anything to regret yet.

Phillip: Speaking of regret, the Yankees spent $120,000,000 on Tanaka and he's injured already. But they like "mature" players ready for the baseball bone yard.

Jeremy: Speaking of mature, how is Ruthie? We haven't seen you guys in a while. Can we do Sunday brunch?

Phillip: "Don't get around much anymore." You know, Ruthie may be right? I've changed and settled for comfort and lack of conflict. Five years married to an attractive, sensual, available woman, and I'm bored. Maybe Bill Maher is right. "It's not rich vs. poor, or beauty vs. not. It's old versus new."

Jeremy: Oh, come on. That's Maher in his narcissistic prick phase. Ten years ago, the old times, you could take a stab at the personals. Now you have to subscribe to a dating service and wait too long for the rush you need. Why bother?

Phillip: As I recall, you weren't very successful at that game either.

Jeremy: Yeah, and later I dropped a few bucks on JDate, but they all wanted to get married first and laid later. I'm lucky I met

LoRita. [On the bar is a complimentary copy of the *Village Voice*. In fact, all copies of the *Voice* are complimentary.]

Jeremy: You know, the *Voice* always has ads for immediately available shrinks, masseurs, and personals for people of every stripe. [He reads from the *Voice*] *GWM, 37, in fashion. Looking for someone healthy and successful to adore. Older is OK.*

Phillip: Too threatening, and I can't afford to be a sugar daddy. Especially for a guy.

Jeremy: *BWF Teacher, 45. Someone sensitive who cares and enjoys the beach, dining, etc..*

Phillip: La-dee-dah.

Jeremy: Well, here's a candidate. *GWF, 27. I can party and I can dance. but the best is soul: music, kisses, everything.*

Phillip: She sounds hot. Here goes. [He dials her number] Hello. My name is Phil and I'm calling in response to your ad in the *Voice*.

Maxine: I'm Maxine. And you're calling about meeting me? What for? And what's your name again?

Phillip: Phil, and I'm an editor—

Maxine: Wait a minute, Phil. Are you one of those jerks who's so in love with your prick that he wants to turn gays like me into straights?

Phillip: No, I can't help my gender, but—

Maxine: Lemme ask you two questions. Do men like it when women make a lot of noise during sex?

Phillip: Oh, definitely.

Maxine: And do women like it as much when men make noise?

Phillip: Sure.

Maxine: See, you're a fraud, and you don't understand women, straight or gay. We don't need the sound effects. So, Mister Bullshit Artist with the magic dick, goodbye! [She slams down the phone.]

Phillip: That was really harsh, but maybe she has a point Let's try one more.

Jeremy: *GBF, 37, executive looking for a woman of substance. Must like Ramones, Werner Herzog, and all cuisines. Well-traveled.*

Phillip: Now, there's someone cool. The Ramones and a little weed. Skip the Werner Herzog. Here's a smart woman perhaps with a nice round ass. What more could you ask for?

Jeremy: One problem. She's another lesbian. You must be a glutton for punishment.

Phillip: Here's a different approach. I'll pretend to be a female. I failed as a male, but this is different, and maybe I can strike up a conversation as a woman. If I can turn on a straight female as a guy, maybe I can turn on a lesbian as a female. Different. A real challenge. Something new.

Jeremy: What's the matter with you? Too many Guinnesses? You've been married for five years, and perhaps you can't keep it in your pants any longer? But this? Acting like a lesbian to seduce a lesbian? You are in way over your head.

Phillip: Look who's talking! If I keep my voice high I can sound like a woman. I said respond to me, not marry me. It's an experiment. A goof. I may even learn something.

Jeremy: You're going to end up as a gay guy, for Chrissake.

Phillip: Being a seductress to another female? The idea tickles my fancy. But I'm going to see if Ruth and LoRita can give me helpful hints on what to say. See you at brunch Sunday.

Jeremy: You better tickle something else. Who are you going to be? Phyllis? Jeanie? And what about her feelings, or Ruth's? I really hope nothing comes of this. It's getting too weird, and I'm going home. But judging from the past, you're not going to listen to me.

Act 1, Scene 3: Phillip, Jeremy, Ruth,
and LoRita at brunch at the bar–restaurant.

Ruth: I hate some of the recent changes swamping us. Ten years ago it was *croque monsieur, croque* everywhere for brunch. Now it's pig's cheeks, bacon, trotters. I think it's unconscious anti-Semitism.

Jeremy: Relax. Today is today. Eat your veggies and pretend to be happy as a locavore.

Phillip: Can we be serious for a minute? More than food, I'm curious about changes in the present roles of men and women. Can a man understand a woman, or was Gloria Steinem right when she said, "A woman without a man is like a fish without a bicycle."

LoRita: Sounds like you're bicycling, or just bi today.

Phillip: I'm trying to come to grips with the end of the days of male dominance. [to Ruth] For example. What attitude and words turned you on when we met, and is it different now?

LoRita: Oh, boy! What brings you to this quest for enlightenment?

Ruth: That's easy to answer. First I like to be pursued, chased, and feel hot breath on my neck. I want my man to come after me. That was basic then and it is now.

Phillip: I always wondered if that was crude or off-putting.

Ruth: Without the right words, it might have become that, but I liked having my buttons pushed. Glad you asked.

Phillip: But what about oral sex or anal sex?

LoRita: Down, boy. Easy. We haven't even eaten brunch.

Ruth: Well, I figured I should do whatever pleased my man, and frankly it gave me a sense of power and control. You never pulled nasty surprises, and I could steer your response. You respected what I didn't like, which was not much, but I miss the old hunter. It seems like caution has become the order of the day.

Phillip: But I'm more curious about the words. What did I say that turned you on? Or off? And is it the same now? What are the magic words? What would I say to stoke a woman's desires?

Jeremy: That's a mouthful.

Phillip: I am just trying to get a picture of what it was like for Ruth or women in general.

Jeremy: Over brunch?

Ruth: I like the topic so far, if it's not too hot for you guys. There were comments like "Nice dress," "You look really terrific tonight," that tickled impulses for something later. Subtle. Courting my response. Comments about tits and ass don't work, though they seem to come pretty naturally to you. And you don't do this anymore, but comments about money and my income felt intrusive. I want to be desired for myself.

LoRita: *Brava. Brava!*

Phillip: I've got to say that what made you feel more like a woman made me feel more like a man. Do you think that's eternal?

Ruth: Yes.

Jeremy: Yes.

LoRita: Yes.

Ruth: Let's order.

Act 2, Scene 1: Phillip is calling from the bar. Chondra is in her apartment; sleek, modern, elegant. This their first conversation.

Phillip: Hi. This is Phyllis. I'm responding to your personal ad in the *Village Voice*. I always look for a special connection with a new friend, and you mentioned some of my favorite entertainment. I love the Ramones and did you see Werner Herzog's movie *Boyhood*? I really long for an intelligent friendship and, if it goes well, much more. But first I have to get to know you. Will you talk with me?

Chondra [coolly]: You know it's customary to first make contact through the newspaper. This is a bit intrusive. How do I know who you really are? For Chrissake, your voice sounds like a *man's*.

Phillip: No, no, I'm Phyllis. It's been a long time between meaningful relationships—

Chondra [interrupting]: Phyllis, I already have friends and colleagues in droves. If you're looking for someone to go to the movies with, I don't go to the movies, I finance them. And

Boyhood is crap. On the other hand, I don't have an active sexual partner so, yes, I'm interested.

Phyllis: Well, I was wondering if—

Chondra [interrupting]: I don't know what you need or want, but sex is highest on my list. That's my agenda. Up front.

Phillip: Of course, but I need to *feel* something before having sex. Aren't you rushing it? I don't even know your last name.

Chondra: Names aren't the issue. What do you look like? Tall, slender, nice legs, no tits? Urban chic is OK. Buxom and a bit of a babe? I could make that rhyme sing. Or maybe you're short, dumpy, and nondescript. There can be a real fire under that plain cover, and I'm the gal to ignite it.

Phillip: Why do people always concentrate on looks first? Since they are obviously so important to you, I'm of average height, and I have a deep, almost masculine voice, but most people consider me to be something of a looker and, yes, sexy.

Chondra: That sounds amazing, but you aren't even on Facebook. My mystery girl. I like that. Let me explore your mind. What are you reading now?

Phillip :Oh, the basics. Betty Freidan, Rita Brown, Gloria Steinem, Simone de Beauvoir.

Chondra: Honey, I read those guys a long time ago. What are you, a missionary-position type flat on your back while they pump you fill of ideas? How about Mujares Creando? Or Michelle Goldberg, or Tina Vasquez? *They're* the ones who are searching for something other than yesterday's answers.

Phillip: I read Horace Mann's book about a man and a boy in Venice. They could be two women.

Chondra: Oh, boy. It's Thomas Mann. Forget about whether the characters have dicks or not, and think of the courage it took to feel that, to write that, to welcome that, to grasp that passion.

Phillip: I'm confused. I thought you were just a lesbian.

Chondra: Honey, I'm not just *anything*. I'm everything. But I have to go. Do you want to call or meet tomorrow? This was a good start.

Phillip: Can I call after 10:00 p.m.?

Chondra: OK. Goodbye, Phyllis.

*Act 2, Scene 2: One week later. Chondra is in her
apartment, and Phillip is on his cellphone in the bar.*

Chondra: Hi, beautiful. Did you have a great day? You are really such a tease. Even though I'm not seeing or touching you yet, just thinking of you makes me wet.

Phillip [dramatically]: *Oooh!*

Chondra: Open up your bra and touch your breasts.

Phillip: *Ooooooh!*

Chondra: Now slide your hands into your panties.

Phillip: *Oooh. Ohh.*

Chondra: Do you know how much I want to see you, to have you?

Phillip: Can't you feel what's happening inside me? I've never imagined anyone who could reach me this way. I feel like a different person. I'm consumed with you. I'm so lucky!

Chondra: There are so many more wonderful ways I could make you feel. In just one week your deep voice and femininity are driving me crazy.

Phillip: Everything is so intense. I feel so hot. I can't wait to get together, but I'm so afraid of disappointing you. To see in your eyes, "This is it?" Let's just have our passion on the phone. It's safer. No heartbreak.

Chondra: Screw safety. I've got to see you. I'm crawling with desire but my patience has its limits. I haven't felt this way in years. It's *passion*. It's *love!*

Phillip: Please don't be angry. I'm frightened. [He is sweating profusely.] I feel like a little boy—er, girl.

Chondra: No, it's got to be now. Give me a time and a place, or it's over. I can't feel this way and wait forever.

Phillip: How can I decide?

Chondra: Time and place, time and place.

Phillip: Raoul's this Sunday at 8:00 PM. I know you from Facebook, and you can't miss me. Let's not talk for the next few days. until Sunday night. By then I'll be on fire.

Chondra: Me, too. Me, too. But skip the restaurant, and meet me at my apartment.

Phillip: OK. Your place. Night!

Chondra: Night! I'll have a surprise.

Phillip [aside] :What have I done?

Act 2, Scene 3: Phillip and Jeremy
in the Chelsea bar one day later.

Phillip: Help me, Jeremy. I started out playing a game, and now I'm twisted and trapped. I feel awful. It's not a goof anymore. It's become real, and I have a date in person with Chondra.

Jeremy: You *should* feel rotten. You got this woman passionately involved thinking you are a female, but you're a fraud and she just called your bluff. I'm more worried about her feelings than about yours. Well, you caught your fish. Now what do you do?

Phillip: I know. I know. Chondra is so much fun, so outspoken and brave, and still attentive to my wishes. This will break her heart. I'm already broken-hearted. I can't help myself anymore. I'm such a creep.

Jeremy: Asshole is more like it.

Phillip: And that's not the worst part. I'm. . .I'm in *love* with her. She touches me in a way that no other person has. I feel myself opening and closing with her spirit inside my soul [gestures dramatically].

Jeremy: Jesus Christ, you've flipped. Flipped into what I don't know. So I guess now you're a woman trapped in a man's body. I need another beer.

Phillip: I'm *something* trapped in a man's body. and I don't know what is to become of me. I can't bear to think of telling Ruth.

Jeremy: Oh, incidentally, while your great transformation is going on, can you still get it up with Ruth, or is that too ordinary for you now?

Phillip: You know that, despite my feelings for Chondra and my new awareness about myself, Ruth and I have had more and better sex in the past two weeks than in years. Her body is driving me crazy.

Jeremy: Phillip, Phillip, how are you going to tell Ruth? She'll be crushed, or maybe she'll just throw you out and you can continue your experiment with Chondra.

Phillip: Well I'd better tell her soon. Our first in-person meeting is Sunday. There are two women in my life and I'm going to betray them both.

Jeremy: I think there are *three* women in your life now, and that is two too many. One would be the right number, but I'm still your friend, Phil. . .or is it Phyllis?

Phillip: I'll tell Ruthie tonight.

*Act 2, Scene 4: Phillip and Ruth at home
that night. Phillip is pacing.*

Phillip: Ruth, we have to have a serious talk about something we've never confronted before. [Phillip fixes a drink.]

Ruth: OK, but can we screw first? I'm restless.

Phillip: Ruth, I'm in deep trouble, and it's all my fault, and it'll surely hurt you deeply. God, I'm so *sorry*.

Ruth: You creep. Who is she? We've been swinging from the chandelier, having the greatest sex of our marriage, and now you drop this on me. Fuck you.

Phillip: No, no, it's not what you think. Nobody's pregnant, and I'm not dating anyone. I love you. You can ask Jeremy.

Ruth: I'm asking *you*. Did you lose money gambling? Did you join the Mafia? Are you turning gay or [she holds her head] Republican? I know Obama's been a disappointment, but you didn't have to go that far. Whatever it is, it didn't just happen. What did you do?

Phillip: Well, Jeremy and I were reading the ads, the personals, in the *Village Voice*. . . .

Ruth: Spare me, little boy.

Phillip: We were half drunk, and I decided to answer an ad pretending to be a lesbian courting another lesbian.

Ruth: Is this for real? And who the hell do you think you are? Playing a woman in love with another woman! You've never felt the power of sex between two women. Each tongue and hand know just where to go. And you don't know the tenderness and communication, the opening and closing. . . .

Phillip: And you do?

Ruth [after a long pause]: As long as we're into truth and consequences, I did it a couple of times in college, but it was just an experiment. I'm not really a lesbian, and I love you—wait a minute, why am *I* apologizing?

Phillip: Do you still think of women even when we're doing it?

Ruth: Yes, I still think of women, but no, not when we're doing it. What's the rest of your story? So far it's just you and Jeremy being the usual assholes.

Phillip: I started calling this woman, Chondra, who's thirty-seven and gay—

Ruth [interrupting]: Get to the point. Somehow I can't believe what I'm hearing.

Phillip: We've talked a half-dozen times, and she's really smitten with me.

Ruth: But you haven't seen her, and she doesn't know you have a dick?

Phillip: Even worse, she's doing strange things to me. I talk differently with her, and I have different feelings. You know what you said about tongues and tits. . .well—

Ruth [interrupting]: Tongues and hands.

Phillip: Well, I'm beginning to feel that way, and it scares the hell out of me.

Ruth: It certainly hasn't hurt your performance in bed.

Phillip [dramatically]: No, but sometimes when we're together I feel like I'm you and me at the same time. I'm so fucked up.

Ruth: Fucked up is the phrase. If you're suffering that much, why don't you just ditch her? Does she know your name?

Phillip: Just my cell phone, but I can't just run away. I hate the thought of hurting her, but I have to see her in person.. I'm still curious. It's like I'm drugged. . .or infected.

Ruth: Stick with drugged. Infected is worse. You've never actually met her?

Phillip: No, no.

Ruth: Well, to tell the truth, I'm a little curious, too. I've got to see this for myself. Just so she doesn't faint when she finds out that Phyllis is a prankster with a penis, I'll go along to help pick up the pieces. In fact, I'll talk to Jeremy and LoRita. You'll have three people to support you and create a distraction. When is the meeting?

Phillip: 8:00 PM Sunday.

Act 2, Scene 5: Chondra's apartment.
She answers the bell for the foursome.

Chondra: Hello. This is a surprise. [Looks at Ruth] Phyllis, you're beautiful.

Ruth: Not me. I'm Phyllis's wife, Ruth. He's Phyllis [points to Phillip].

Phillip: [Stricken, he falls to his knees] I'm Phyllis. . .and I'm—I'm so *sorry*. I played a terrible trick to see if I could attract a woman while playing a woman. Then I got really involved in being Phyllis and immensely moved by our relationship. Oh my God, I am so sorry. I feel totally confused.

LoRita: Phillip, do you have sex with men, too?

Phillip: No. . .no.

LoRita: Just asking.

Chondra: I didn't think there were *any* new stories out there. Of course I'm angry and very disappointed. My hopes were very high. I now know Phyllis—you don't mind if I call you Phyllis for a while—and Ruth—but who are *they*? [Gestures toward Jeremy and LoRita.]

Jeremy: Jeremy.

LoRita: And LoRita. We're friends who came along to pick up the pieces if necessary.

Chondra: Thanks, but as long as I know who *I* am, I'll be OK. [To Phillip] Phyllis, where did you come up with this game?

Phillip: I'm so sorry. It was meant to be a gag, but it's become so much more to me.

Ruth [shouting at Phillip]: *Gag?* You *asshole*. You have no idea how powerful sex is in a woman. Chondra is the only honest person here. And from now on I'll never know *who* I'm having sex with. Now *I'm* confused!

Jeremy: I'm beginning to think it doesn't matter. Twiddle this, twiddle that, it's just who you are tonight.

Chondra: Well, I've twiddled almost everything, and I think I know what's best for me. [Looks at Ruth] Can I freshen your drink?

Ruth: [looks down coyly] Tonight has certainly given heterosexuality a black eye. I think we should all appreciate Chondra. She knows what's real, honest, and irresistible.

Jeremy: Yeah.

LoRita: Yes.

Phillip: I'll always remember you as a wonderful person, Chondra, but we've got to go. I can't believe how much you *got* to me.

Chondra: [Hugs Ruth] Perhaps we'll meet again. Goodbye, Phillip. You're forgiven.

Act 2, Scene 6: Six months later.
Phillip and Jeremy in the bar.

Jeremy: What do you hear from Ruth these days?

Phillip: Not much. She's moved in with Chondra and taken all her stuff. I guess the best man won.

Jeremy: Or something like that. I knew this would lead to trouble, and now I even worry about LoRita sometimes.

Phillip: Look at these. [He holds up a copy of the *Voice* personals] *GWM, BBF, Baltic contortionist, luscious tranny.* Something for everyone but me.

Jeremy: Don't worry. Someone will come along.

Phillip: [Still quoting the *Voice*] *Diana, the Huntress, desires adventurous female. I will teach you the chase and I will be your Dark Protector. Thirties only.*

Phillip: Oooh...Ooooooh. [There is a long pause as he picks up the phone and the curtain descends.]

Chapter Two

LIGHTNING

I MET JACKSON IN FIRST GRADE. At the start of the year, as I remember, we were both a little afraid. At least I was. The teacher, Mrs. Abernathy, was nice, and the kids all got along with one another. Soon I was looking forward to school. Jackson and I hit it off because we lived three blocks apart and many days walked home together. In gym, we were the two fastest boys, and that put us at the top of a list. So far as I knew we were all mostly the same, learning to recognize words and read.

Jackson missed a week of school just before Christmas vacation. Kids get sick, then they get well. So it was no big deal. But something really different had happened to Jackson. All of a sudden he could read and do math, even long division. He was reading adventure books and sports books. He would try to talk to me about these topics, but they were way over my head. Oddly, he hadn't developed physically. He was the same size as me and didn't run faster or catch a ball better. But he was a whole lot smarter.

When you're a kid you just accept mysteries like that. It was enough of a task to understand my mother telling me to dress warmer. Then, year after year, until the summer after fourth grade, I grew smarter and Jackson stayed the same. Looking back, I might have been more curious about him but we grew physically at the same rate and still played together once in a while. Strangest of all, over the next three school years I caught up with him, and by fourth grade we were even in schoolwork.

Then, over the summer it happened again. I started fifth grade, and Jackson was years ahead of all of us. I had made it through Dr. Seuss all the way to Hardy Boys, but he was reading Clair Bee sports books. He was the same kid when we played little league baseball and could still talk a little about sports. But what really puzzled me was how much he talked about his body and other kids' appearance.

What was the problem? Neither one of us was getting bullied, at least physically. Perhaps Jackson bullied us in class by suddenly being way smarter. But he didn't mean to rub it in. Besides, he was always insecure about his body. He worried about having muscles, and he was always focused on "What do they think of me?" He blushed around Jane Dickens because he liked her. But his body was, in fact, no different from those of the rest of us. Just his brain was different. Bigger. Smarter.

Then it happened a third time. I and most of my friends had caught up academically.

By eighth grade graduation we were getting the same grades, wearing the same size clothes, and worrying about the things that Jackson had agonized over for four years. We were friends and equals again. Or partners in misery.

I still remember ninth grade a little like kindergarten. It was pretty heavy until I got my footing. It was then that I recognized that Jackson was truly different. He had jumped again, and it was like he had finished high school over the summer. He talked about politics, writers, and thankfully, sports. What we had in common was sports, especially baseball, and acne, cracking voices, and long, stringy arms and legs. I don't think it helped him much that he had already been through the muscle-watching, penis-measuring stage. By the time we were ready to actually talk to girls and not just talk about them, he was already worrying about cars and college, while we were still shedding our bicycles.

Again, over the next four years I caught up and we graduated together. To my surprise we both enrolled in the same college. I was in engineering, and he was in psychology. He must have known that he needed some psychological help figuring out what kept happening. Soon after freshman orientation, I got the fourth shock of our friendship. Jackson was some kind of genius again. And this time we were on opposite sides of the Earth. Frankly, I was pissed. I was a freshman, and he was mentally a senior ready to graduate. Finally, I asked him, "Jackson, what is it with you? Every four years you're suddenly miles ahead of me. It's just not normal and it's kind of hard to take."

"I don't know," he said. "I just don't know. It's not that I want it, it just happens. If I could stop it, I would." Once again, time was the great equalizer. We spent several years in different spheres academically and socially, but by graduation we were getting back together as friends and equals. I now regret that I didn't push my question harder, but I was intimidated.

Several years passed before we met again. We were twenty-five, and I had to get a better explanation. I pressed him. I'd never hurt him or envied his leaps forward. Now. in the name of friendship, I had to know.

Nothing could have prepared me for his response.

"I've wanted to tell somebody outside of my family all my life. I'm. . .I'm a freak. I take no credit for my great leaps forward. In each case I was hit by lightning, and when I came to, my brain was different. See? See? You're smiling. I knew it! I hate it, and I hate myself. There's a crack of thunder, and twenty minutes later I wake up, burned foot and hand, head and chest, hair and eyebrows singed and the most awful headache imaginable. Four times my parents took me to doctors, who confirmed the event. After the second strike, we lived in astraphobia—terror about lightning. We listened to dozens of weather reports each day trying to anticipate storms. Will it keep happening? How could I have survived four strikes? Where could I hide? You know my life mostly has been better than good, but the weird leaps in intellect have also made *me* uncomfortable. And I could never tell anyone. The only people who know are my parents, doctors. . .and, now, you. Do you think I'm lying? Or crazy?"

It was an amazing story, and I struggled to grasp what he had told me. His whole life had been dominated by four bolts of lightning, each of which should have killed him. I felt intensely on the spot for a response. "Jackson, I never heard or imagined anything like this. Lightning hit you four times, and you survived them all? That's why you were so smart?" Frankly, I was still envious. I could imagine girls crawling all over him like he was some kind of celebrity. Captain Lightning. "We're friends and we always will be," I said, embracing him. But I was thinking, *This is too far out! But how did he make such leaps in brain power? I've got to keep in touch.*

We started different careers. He chose finance and, fueled by a fifth strike just before he began work, was a *wunderkind*. He was rich by age thirty, and I was still a junior engineer. Still, as in the past, I was catching up. He was a man in a hurry about life. He had married and had a child on the way. He was already wealthy, but as you can imagine, he was still haunted. *Will there be more? When? Will I survive? Will I see my child graduate college?* And, of course, *Why?* the most devastating question of all. He had never told his wife. He had met her on an emotional high after his first post-college lightning strike, number five. Only I and his doctors knew, and I bet they didn't actually believe him.

Lightning stuck him next at age forty-six. He had gone twenty years, time enough to raise a family and have a career. Maybe it was a reprieve from God, but fate always collects its dues. During a visit to his son at college, he was hit while standing under a tree with his wife and child. The strike knocked him unconscious, blew off a shoe, and burned his left shoulder and right foot. His wife commented on his seeming calm after the drama, and he decided to keep his secret. But after a twenty-year hiatus, the seal had been broken.

All the questions I had raised twenty years before sprang to life. His mood darkened, and brooding became a painful fact of everyday life. He had aged another ten years from the strike and suffered the added indignity of encroaching fragility. After forty, we make no great advances in our knowledge or wisdom, but age and fear take root. Here was a forty-year-old man in a fifty-year-old body. Would the next bolt push him over the edge?

It was hard to doubt the veracity of his story. His wife and child, and several doctors from his pediatrician up, had seen him and marveled at his survival. So did I. It was not my finest hour, but I slowly began to edge away. I, too, was forty-six and didn't like the sound of footsteps. I had two small children and a lot to accomplish.

So I progressed while Jackson began to crumble. His solitary brooding ruined his marriage, and he had only a tenuous relationship with his son. He had long retired from his lucrative career, but found little joy in anything. He had tried psychotherapy and antidepressants. Nothing worked. He wryly suggested to his psychiatrist that they try electroconvulsive therapy, ECT. The psychiatrist, still in the dark, didn't get the irony.

We met for the last time at our fortieth high school reunion. Attendance was sparse, but Jackson had asked me to come and said he would be there only to see me. I felt guilty enough to go. After all, my life was a happy one. Jackson had recently suffered his seventh lightning strike and, at sixty, was a tired old man with waning intellect. Only his fears, and his consuming rage at the games fate had played with him, survived. He was essentially a lonely eighty-year-old man with his loves, hopes, and accomplishments incinerated by one second of seven hundred- millivolt lightning strikes.

I give the man credit. The next year he took his own life rather than wait. I hope he smiled at finally cheating the lightning gods. Now every storm speaks to me of Jackson.

So I raise my middle finger to the sky and think, "He beat you! He took everything you had, and in the end, he was his own man, making his own fate."

(Roy Sullivan, 1912–1983, holds the Guinness Book records for the most times being hit by lightning. The odds are 10,000-to-one per strike, but Sullivan worked as a U.S. park ranger in hazardous terrain; from 1942 to 1977 he was struck by lightning seven times. All strikes were medically authenticated. He eventually died by his own hand after a romantic disappointment. The protagonist in this story is also hit seven times, but the events are otherwise entirely fictitious.)

Chapter Three

A BIG BREAKFAST

My mother said that breakfast
is the most important meal.
Every day should start with
a big breakfast. So I struggled with
pancakes and hash browns. Then I
discovered a *really* big breakfast.

It is 8:00 AM, and I am sitting
with coffee and you in bedclothes.
Your eyes, green as pears, glisten and beckon.
Your lips are bright berries
ripe for picking. Touching
the soft curve of your neck
makes me hungrier and hungrier.

All of this is prelude to the feasts below.
These are the lands of milk and honey,
the precious body of love
that starts each day. This is the
bounty of a big breakfast, and
everyone's day should know
its reward, including health.
But work and the world will
claim their dues. Trembling and
torn, I dress, pick up the
car keys and glance wistfully
over my shoulder.

"What's for lunch?"

THE WORSHIP OF FOOD

Pursuing the Food of the Moment Trail
There's uni, and seaweed, and kale
Preceding chocolate cake, the new holy grail.

Dover sole, cassoulet, the French palate
Put a sizeable hole in my wallet.
While Henri Soule did his ballet,

Alice Waters peddled the fresh,
California's answer to stress.
If it worked was anyone's guess.

Let me end with martinis, necessarily *gin*.
Please don't put lesser spirits in.
One's for deep talk, the other's a grin.

Is it poetry or food that we crave?
Is it rhyme or a pear for which we slave?
We could be good but we misbehave

around food.

PLAINLY SPEAKING

Plain, as in vanilla, is largely white
with subtle flashes of Tahitian brown
bringing visual stimulation to an otherwise
insipid custard. Plain and simple.

This poem is plain, written in
such language as to be
immediately understood without
references to obscure gods or
tortured takes on nature. Words
and ideas are comprehensible, even simple,
and unfit for publication in the *New Yorker*.

One plane flies at 50,000 feet.
In its silence it brings a
twinge of triumph: "We did it."
We, of course, is *homo sapiens*,
the master of technology.

Another plain lies flat and still,
mute except for conversation
with Ted Kooser. It feeds us,
but who cares ? Deeply
believing in God, Plains people
suffer all the pains of nature.
This plain is anything but predictable.

Another plane, utilitarian in
ugly design, exists only

to shave wood. There's such a plane,
unused, somewhere
in everybody's basement.

My favorite metaphor,
"Plainer than a hen's ass,"
is pure hometown Whitehall,
and totally accurate. Let your
mind roam to hen's asses.
This is plainly the end.

CERVICAL SPONDYLOTIC MYELOPATHY

The pheasant and the mallard duck
have white rings adorning their
necks, insignia of beauty and
sexual appeal to the female.
Parrots and snakes sport colored
rings. Nature loves adornments.

Here is my ring.
A stone necklace now
grows inside my neck.
Bone gently squeezes my
spinal cord, the core of my existence.
My necklace is unseen,
unfelt, and unwanted.

What is perceived emerges distantly.
One toe responds weakly to vibration.
Knee and forearm reflexes over-respond.
Small objects are dropped,
slipping unawares out of hand.
Gait is slinky, narrow, and
unsteady. Unpredictable
wobbles and growing clumsiness
indicate long tract signs,
myelopathy caused by
cervical compression
from my spondylotic necklace.

My spondylosis and I
can share a long future.
As anomalies go,

it's not the worst,
just a secret pain in the neck.

MONDAY TWO TO FOUR
(For our poetry reading group)

We meet every month to nourish the soul
with afternoon snacks to appease the hole
in our stomachs, which, sad to mention,
would otherwise manage to steal our attention.

It's Frost versus fish,
and if I had my wish
I'd pack up the rhyme
and spend all my time,

you know what it means,
and bury myself in a mountain of beans
or peanuts, still in the shuck;
for the parsing of rhyme I don't give a fuck.

We'll give poetry a few more cracks,
then turn to real meaning, the snacks,
and think of what a joy it would be
to add to the menu a cocktail or three.

LAND AHOY

Yesterday we received the Lands' End catalogue,
The newest issue for men and women.
As always, the men stood confident
and at ease: shirts open at the collar and
casual slacks with a perfect drape.
They said, "Buy Lands' End. Look like me."
What pretty girl could resist?
The models' patrician looks promised
riches like ripe peaches to be plucked.
Who wouldn't want to resemble ancestors
who came over on the *Mayflower*? First class!

For four years I tried to grow enough ivy
to conceal my humble Whitehall roots.
I wore chinos, Scottish tweed jackets,
and even smoked a briar pipe.
No one was fooled. "That little Italian boy,"
Paul Keeney called me. I threw up
on him at a black- tie dinner at the Bat Club.
The Bats loved it, and the reward was
three months free dues.
There were ten Finals clubs.
Nine were rich and snooty.
The Bat Club was cheap, down and dirty.
Perfect.

Still, everyone needs clothes, or "threads"
as they were called. So I bought
two button-down Oxford shirts,

one blue and one white, tan corduroy pants,
and six black boxer undershorts.
Models are never shown in boxers. Perhaps
they don't wear anything under that tweed.
Lands' End commando style. Now that's
really over my head. Land ahoy.

Chapter Four

PHYSIOLOGY

Hunger fades.
Satiety's a whore.
Anger relents, and
contentment's no more.

Lust weakens
little by little.
Even trust
rusts like a griddle.

Sadness dissipates
like yesterday's fashion.
Boredom is short,
another dim passion.

Serotonin, GABA, our
neurochemical transmitters,
shift their balances
as our fickle mood flitters.

Mind, then, is mindless
and transient, brief.
Receptors' frail balances
are time's real thief.

So ride the wave gently,
don't struggle and fight.
Today brings pleasure
and tomorrow's a fright.

Give up the falsehood
that willpower's mighty.
Relax and rejoice that
your moods will be flighty—

not eternally dark
or persistently bright,
but always something
just out of sight.

THE GRAND CANYON

It is a magnificent hole, but don't
tremble at the edge of the Grand Canyon.
The dirt could crumble, and your
footing dissolve into free fall.
Equally dangerous is the opposite.
Fear itself causes frozen posture,
leading to loss of small dynamic
adjustments, the basis of balance.

To astrophysicists studying space,
a few pings depict collapsing
galaxies. The black hole is a
gigantic vacuum, consuming
everything and leaving
a ripple in the field of gravity.
Light, time, and gravity are one.
The Grand Canyon is just a speck
inside this massive hole.

Nothing escapes. You and I are bound
for time indescribable
in a manner incomprehensible.
It is frightening, but the
Thought draws you over the edge.

ACROPHOBIA

Something primitive draws me
to look over the edge.
When fear subsides, I
stare into the abyss then
imagine soaring through space,
crashing into the canyon walls,
and coming to rest,
dead, by the side of a river.

THINGS THAT PEEL AWAY

Unfold the rose
sheath by sheath,
red by red,
pink by pink,
smaller and smaller.

Layers yield
to curiosity, the
probe for essence.
So it is with
things that peel.

Promise fires our quest.
Each petal has its
tone, its fragrance,
its fragility, like a
truth enfolded.

In the end, what
have we learned
about the rose,
or all other things
that peel away?

READING ART

Looking through *Art in America*,
the issue featuring Krushenick,
I felt the swarm of the unborn,
struggling fragments of perception
trying to unite and bring something
new, a reality worth looking at.

But the leap from vague concept
to actualizing a perception,
husbanding and mothering an idea
to reality, has many handicaps.
There are too many people around
and no time or privacy for mating.
Worse, ideas are slippery,
my grasp is weak, and the
rare attempt to break the shell
and paint leaves me panting
for technique. Better to write.

Words skip without effort
onto the page. Every color,
every hue, is near at hand.
There is no indecision on the palette.
The paths to connection open wide,
and the promise of completion
comforts from the start.
Language trumps art, but not by much.

JASPER JOHNS' AMERICAN FLAG

Stare head-on at the small
white dot. Linger, second by second,
as green and orange and black
deplete retinal cells. Then
close your lids and await the
innerscape, Old Glory—emerging
art hidden by light.

I want art from within,
where I am artist, canvas, paint— everything.
I stare fixedly at a bright light,
then close my eyelids as Goethe did.
I press until panes of green and deep blue
glow for seconds, then fade to red and violet.
Then darkness comes.

Inner art is more evanescent
than music, more fragile
than poetry, and more
abstract than literature.
Just shut your eyes and see.

Chapter Five

HAIKU (Inside Out)

Autumn murmurs hush
rustling leaves. Everything leads
to silent winter.

QUESTIONS FOR NATURE

February's frozen mazes, trees
blending gray sky to
snow white earth, suffer penance
for the perfumed
days of summer.

Bushes stripped of leaves and berries
huddle under a mantle of snow.
Is their blanket a gift of shelter
from the cold, or merely
another burden?

Can nature, mute and isolated,
comprehend this stolid season?
Does she embrace desolation
as warning that leaves and birdsong
pass to ice?

Does she know that spring
will come, that time plays
many tunes, and everything
lost today in cold will be
revived by sunlight?

EPILOGUE

Can nature see my empathy,
my winter decades long?
Snow, iced over, glistens
under moonlight. After days
of joy, tonight is chill, the
harvest of unspoken guilt.
Will I ever be forgiven
for the wrongs I never did?

RAIN

Today is one of sheets
and drizzles, rain
that oversoaks the ground,
invades the cellar, and
dissolves our resolve
for any productivity.

I see a child, full of
manic delight,
splashing heedlessly in a
puddle. He is the one and only
king of the rain, and
nothing curbs his joy.

After a rainy football
practice, pads heavy
with sweat and water, we
need a steaming shower.
Necessary but mad, the
joy of hot rain is inescapable.

Now, as I watch, the
outside world is in tumult.
School guards, cart boys, and
homeless bums suffer.
I sit peaceful, dry, and
soporific, safe behind walls.

NOW

Poetry is planting flowers
in pitch black. Each word
is soft and sticky, looking
for its partner in harmony.
Purple and gold play with
one another, while orange and
pink strike notes of discord.

Tonight there is no moonlight.
Clouds insure tomorrow will be a
surprise. Is there a grand
happenstance design to be
revealed by daylight? Or was it
random choose-and-plant,
often dug up by tomorrow's dawn?

Which brings me to my body,
where I alone struggle as
dysfunctional gardener.
I hate my body. It is poorly
assembled: too short and
getting shorter, trembling,
and unable to run or jump.

Bit by bit it is turning
pink and orange and purple,
green and brown and blue.
Flaws more than aesthetic make
me struggle for existence.

Let me tolerate descent with
gravity and good humor.

I can still write a poem.

EVERYTHING THAT HAPPENS

By youth, by day,
we break the waves
of sameness to tumble
into new. Fear and
curiosity sing a duet
that provokes variety
and discovery. It's
nothing more than
growing into ourselves.

Now the rents of age
cannot be stitched like
tattered, tired clothes.
Existential unrest
prods us toward peace.
Struggle eases, and
the moon and tides
sweep us gently to
shore—someplace, sometime.

Now stillness fosters solitude,
and the thunder
of butterflies prevails.
Mushroom beauty lies
about, but each day

is a plaintive song.
Adrift, from the back rooms
of my memory, I see,
I exhale, and I find you.

BY THE SEA

Two- or three-year-olds
playing on the beach, still unaware
that nature's way is conflict,
pitch sand against the tide
until they tire and, naturally, leave.
The sea pursues its game,
in and out with them or without.

Cormorants, big-billed air lords,
above, and needle-nosed gar below,
relentlessly scour for small fish.
On land the hyena scavenges and
the anaconda waits languidly
in pursuit of nature's prime directive,
food. Children, you will see.
In nature only the tide ignores
food and points its nose toward
the beach and games.

MILKWEED

Milkweed is the staff of life, food
for the monarch butterfly.
This is milkweed, sustainer
of life. To me, milkweed speaks of a
soft summer afternoon
with lazy breezes on an
idyllic sunlit cornfield outside
Whitehall, New York.

It was 1944, and I was five.
My mother and my aunt, my
lifelines, and I are
in a field of milkweed
where we are gathering
milkweed pappi, the
silken parachutes
crowded inside coarse pods.
Kapok, the weightless
airborne filaments, was sent
to the army for insulation
and to the navy for
flotation pillows.

I, too, was a warrior,
helping our brave troops,
a child of the Greatest Generation.
It was a wonderful day:
the mission, the puffs
sent aloft with a gentle

breath, and the mothers.
America was on the path
to victory, and I was doing
my part. Thank you, milkweed.

FALLING ASLEEP IN THE HOSPITAL

Breath in, ease out.
Breathe in, ease out.
Breathe in, ease out.

It is 2:00 AM and, in aloneness,
thoughts of impending surgery
swirl relentlessly. Novel sounds,
variable light, and, yes,
a low level of pain feed
my chaos, my enemy of sleep.
Thank God for my sleep
apnea machine, which
comforts me with its soft
hissing through my mask.

Breathe in, ease out.
Breathe in, ease out,
Breathe in, ease out.

I have a fear of surrender
and helplessness before the
anticipated anesthesia.

Breathe in, ease out.
Breathe in, ease out.
Breathe in, ease out.

A POEM FOR BOTH OF US

She asked, "Can't you write
a poem that's not
about yourself ?" I sniffed.
"If every poem
is about me, then I have
made the world nonexistent."

After a few seconds of smugness,
I could see it clearly.
Every poem *is* about me.
Even saying it's narcissistic
is narcissistic. But if I say,
"Yes, it's about me, but I
wrote it just to please you.
Is that a poem about you?
Or me? Can't it be about us both?"

MISTER KNOW-IT-ALL

Wine. I knew the ideas,
the tastes, the right words.
Then I met Jon, who drew
spirit from the pulp and
guided wine from the earth
to its conception. Forty years of
coaxing joy from fruit
followed, every glass
a lesson from the grape.

I thought I knew something
about death, first having
observed its gravid power
at eleven years of age.
Now, as my body grows old,
replacing damaged tissue
more slowly each year,
I see, from my thinning skin
and shrinking muscles,
a new appreciation of
the ancient road to death.

I thought I knew love,
Mr. Nineteen-Year-Old
Know-It-All—I read
all about it. Then I
met you, and every corner
of my being glistened
with desire and joy.
This is the love that has

led me through life,
and I am still learning
about this gift that
grows all life long.

Chapter Six

DUSK

Crepuscular animals
live in three realms.
One foot lies in daylight,
one in night;
the rest lies in transition.

Owls, blinking majesties,
arouse for daily
feeding on field mice.
Deer forage at dusk,
their luminous eyes blankly
staring at my headlights.
Trout, of another habitat,
covet rising mayflies
dancing in waning light.

These creatures celebrate
the arrival of dusk, while
a shadow grows inside me.
Fading taste and hearing,
hardened corneas,
and mental misfires
hint at dimming times.

Could someone please
leave the light on
just a little longer?

RETIREMENT

Chewing the bitter rind of oranges,
listening for the polyphonic voices
of the past, I try to regress.
But it is only a poem. I am writing
a poem, and it opens no doors.

There was Kathy, whose therapy
was a handful of razor blades
and who lived several years
on the brink of self- extinction.
She triumphed to have love and children.

Another Kathy worked relentlessly but
unsuccessfully trying to neuter her therapy.
After four years I relented and finally
embraced *DSM-IV*, the psychiatric code
that predicts failure and offers absolution.

The strands of events become a fabric
and the intellectual fun of deconstruction,
history and diplomacy fade, and most of all
the trust that fueled insight becomes history.
A kiss to the diaspora who have
graced my professional life.

I WANT TO LEAVE YOU

I want to leave you
music, laughing children,
beads of passion
strung through time,
beach days, and memories
of a beautiful life together.

I want to leave you
knowing, as a wife,
your care, your wit,
your words and intimacies,
and, yes, your pilgrim soul
have been my steel, soufflé, my life.

I want to leave you
saying, No one,
no thing, no love
that I'd imagined
could approach that
which you've brought to me forever.

SUTTEE OF MY HEART

*(The Hindu custom of suttee, now banned, encourages
the wives of high caste to join their husbands on the
funeral pyre. In this poem, the man joins his lost love.)*

Why this mournful burning?
Husbands don't do this.
They don't have to
prove their love twice.
Climbing the funeral pyre
seems undignified,
perhaps insincere.
Let loneliness
thrive in darkness.

So I was sad and quiet.
Then something arose from deep inside,
unbidden and spontaneous.
Now, six weeks later,
ventricles, atria, and coronaries are in flames.
Suttee of my heart,
we are still one.

SEASONS

The words
come freely
on days when

all the world is green blue gold
with aqua and orange sunsets
making waves of joy unfold.

When October days bring cerulean skies,
or April's rain drives tulips high,
then the world echoes nature's primal cry:

"Grow young and strong and shed
the shell that binds you to dread.
Rejoice to be alive." Instead

some would focus solely on the end,
life and death as enemies, not as one
in harmony, and then you can't pretend

the grave is soft
and warm and
welcoming.

THE BURNING HOUR

Each day I feel the
nearness of the burning hour—
not with fear, for that would be
betrayal of our love.

Time is the ruler,
and all loves and dreams
will become treasures
to be left at the gate.

I will lie patient and still
within the boundaries of our chalice,
awaiting the second burning
which will make us one again.

Don't hurry. We'll have
a million lifetimes more.
Don't think of me as gone;
think of me as waiting.

ABOUT THE AUTHOR

Michael R. Milano, M.D., is a recently retired psychiatrist who spent his adult life raising four wonderful children in Teaneck, New Jersey. The love of words started with patrons of his mother's beauty parlor reading to him. It caught fire at Harvard College, but the writing of poetry was an outgrowth of the previously mentioned poetry reading group (Monday Two to Four). Poetry is his vehicle for the expression of love and loss. Add some humor, and you have *Milkweed*.

CPSIA information can be obtained at www.ICGtesting.com
Printed in the USA
BVOW02s0903220816

459698BV00071B/158/P